The Colours of the Clouds

DEBOPRIYA B MUKHERJEE

BlueRoseONE.com
Stories Matter
NewDelhi • London

BLUEROSE PUBLISHERS
India | U.K.

For permissions requests or inquiries regarding this publication, please contact:

BLUEROSE PUBLISHERS
www.BlueRoseONE.com
info@bluerosepublishers.com
+91 8882 898 898
+4407342408967

ISBN: 978-93-6261-787-3

Cover Design: Sadhna Kumari
Typesetting: Pooja Sharma

First Edition: April 2024

PREFACE

Hello Readers! I am Debopriya. This is the first collection I would like to represent in front of you. My book THE COLOURS OF THE CLOUD is all about the different shades of life. Life is like a river that always blows in an unusual flow. The way is not predicted every time. It deposits many feelings, emotions, sensations, and filters. We are wise when we accept the different shades of life. Life appears to us like a color palate where many colors are kept in different segments, sometimes it gets mixed and makes a rainbow and sometimes it reflects its color. Anyway, it is beautiful by every means.

The Colours of the Clouds is completely written in English and a very short and simple sentence pattern has been used to make it readable in front of all types of readers. As an author I expect my readers can relate their different aspects of feelings with the stories.

The Colours of Clouds is all about the journey and acceptance of the different people of different ages. Emotion is quite emphasized here than the social series of do and do not. I will be happy if my readers feel of being of themself while in daylight, we get tired of acting as the slaves of our social identity.

`THE COLOURS OF THE CLOUD' IS DEDICATED TO MY DAUGHTER RUDRA, MY HUSBAND DIPANJAN, MY STUDENTS, AND MY FRIENDS WHO MOTIVATED ME TO PUSH MY LIMITS BEYOND THE BAR ALWAYS.

ABOUT THE AUTHOR

Born on: 10th January 1987, in Chin Surah West Bengal

Education: Master in English language and literature.

Global Certification on Childhood Special Education.

Passion: Writing since the year of 1992. Worked as a student representative, and wrote in little magazines. The first publication was THE SILENT SHADOW, which was an Epublished collection.

Profession: Worked as an English Educator long Eleven years. Presently working with Editech Private LTD as a Research Content Writer.

ACHIEVEMENTS: State-level Essay Competition Winner.

The author is staying in Pune currently.

CONTENTS

THE COLOURS OF THE CLOUDS

The river was not finding its peace in the long run.It was sounding fluttering utter one step, two steps. The sky poured the color of egg yolk into the stretched serine body of the river. The west cloud clotted black and stony bluish. All of a sudden from the green dark forest the heart-rending harsh sound of peacocks came out. A little bursting sound of clustering clouds howled in a low suppressed voice. It was approaching monsoon. The north wind hustled a gust of whimsical clouds. Nil was observing every bit of it from his mountain-facing balcony. He planned a long back to read the book Meghdutt by the great poet Kalidasa in this monsoon. His recent posting to the hill station aggravated his urge over his long-cherished dream. There was hardly a drop or two of rain. He didn't make a single minute late to make a cup of tea, sitting in his balcony coach which was as broken as his old quarter of British period. At last, the time came "kaschit kanta biraha guruna sadhikara parramatta"...A prince of heaven (Yakhha) neglected his duties when he was intoxicated in the indulgence with his beloved, The richest God Kubera cursed him to abandon his luxury and exiled him to the Mountain of Chitrakuta, Ramagiri Ashram. He was alone. He was lonely. He was suffering out of love. Only the great celestial tree of Rudraksha shaded him like his beloved……Tak! Tak!... The door was getting knocked and Nil came out of the pages from Meghdutt. Nil opened the door. 'Harihar…you? At this time? 'Harihar entered the room without any permission. His eyes started to check every nook and corner of the room. And with a hissing voice, he replied 'Yes… it's me. Kushan had sent me to take care of you.

Especially to take care of you and your mind…Ha!!'.Harihar's voice was sarcastic. Nil understood. Nil Joseph Kurian. He was from Kerala. Nil had lost his father when he was eight. Her mother used to supply flowers to their local Church. When Nil was a grade tenth student he got a part-time job in the Churchyard marketplace. A good reputed Innkeeper appointed him to send different bus stops to collect the customers from there. One day he met a huge personality who came out of a huge white Mercedes. The man was wearing blue glasses and a blue suit. Nil was buying paan from the shopkeeper. The man came and lightened his cigar. Removed his glass and asked Nil directly….' Hey boy! Will you work for me? Nil was feeling shy in front of the magnificent personality. 'Will you work for me? 'He asked again. By a meaningful gesture he took Nil towards the big Deodar tree.'...but ..my Inn Keeper has given me some advance! 'The man snatched the word from Nil.' and how much is that? I will give you three months in advance. You will get your accommodation, and payment also triple. What else do you want, boy? 'This time Nil opened his mouth…'My name is Nil, Sir'....'I don't mind whoever you are! You just have to work for me. I will make you rich.' Nil had his lunch an hour before. He just burped and asked 'What do I have to do Sir?'...The huge white Mercedes took both of them inside. Kushan Kanti Agarwal was an ill-famous agent of drugs and an illegal owner of two gold mines. Nil was appointed as the supervisor of his new godown where all the illegal transactions were meant to happen. Nil grew up under opulence, money, and power better to be called a dark world. He was intelligent enough to utilize his brain power to uplift Kushan Kanti more and more.

Harihar entered Nil's balcony. The Meghdutt was still lying down open in the broken coach. The newly approaching rain had aggravated its speed a little bit. On the balcony, the white pure buds of jasmines were beautifully waiting to bloom. The half-dried trees of the lawns had started to emit the strange muddy smell of the drenched ground. Harihar took the book and threw it at the corner of the balcony and raised his voice "Nilu bhai, where are the accounts of the last month's transactions? Those bloody morons!! they took one extra carton of gold bars!!! I swear, I will kill those bastards! Show me the transactions bhai, right now. Nil throws his leftover coffee in the kitchen sink, puts some water over his face and brings the register. Both of them spent the whole evening at work transactions. Nil wanted to have some soup at night but as usual, his wish was all in vain. Harihar took the Zeep and bought some chicken starters. Nil never liked to drink much. He took just a chilled beer. Harihar became drunk within an hour and went to sleep in Nil's bed. Nil knew it very well it was meant to happen. Harihar came here to make his life unbearable even in Matheran. Matheran is a half-dense forest. The monsoon is heavy here. Nil accepted his exile by Kushan Agarwal not only because of his relationship with Mandira but to celebrate his long cherished dream to read Meghdutt in a calm cozy nature. Nil inherited the artistic self of his father from his childhood. He was a talented painter and managed to carry on by anyway. He was not aware of his sprouted artistic self exactly but the nights, when Kushan's people used to murder, the rest of the night he plunged into his palette and colors to believe from the core of his heart that he was none other than an artist. The next very morning his people could see a beautiful picture that was extremely expressive and enlivened.

Once Harihar slept, Nil silently came out of the room. He turned on the dim yellow bulb of his balcony and picked the Meghaduta with a gentle care when the northwest side clouds made a sudden thunder.The thin line of thunder was spreaded through a deep dark horizon...' Asharasaya prathama divase meghamaslishta sanung...bapra krira parinata gaja, prekhaniyang dadarsha'''...At the very first month of Ashara (Approaching monsoon) the Yaksha person observed a piece of huge cloud embracing the mountain in a playful method like a baby elephant....' simple but wonderful, isn't it? Nil thought for a while when he read a few more lines once more. Nil sat on the couch, stretched his whole body, and started to remember Mandira again. Meghdutt reminded him of Mandira time and again. Mandira only suggested that he should have read this Sanskrit Classic. It was Mandira's favorite. The north wind had started to blow and burst till the never-ending tears of Mandira. Mandira was sacred like a dew drop and was deeply loved by Nil. Kushan I kidnapped Mandira when she was a teenage girl. Nil was sitting beside the driver. He was just wondering where from the groaning sound was coming. He used to look after the delivery transactions of the gold mine. He did not know anything about the girl-selling business of Kushan Agarwal. Their gang used to kidnap and supply girls regularly. Nil didn't know where they picked Mandira from but she was able to hear her groaning. Harihar was driving the car.' Can you stop the car nonsense? And tell me what is happening here? 'Nil shouted. Harihar whistled and looked at the back seat. His gesture was unpleasant. Nil jumped into the back seat and released the girl from the tight wrap of the black sack. Holy shit!! It was a young, fresh girl. Soft, supple, deer-eyed, dark black curly hair, a lifeful girl who was shivering like a fragile plant in the upcoming trouble situation in her life. 'You bustard Hari! What is your plan? Tell me now. Why did you pick this girl?' Nil burst into a blind rage. Hari didn't even bother to react. Suddenly from the back seat, a sound of vomiting came out. Nil didn't wait for a single moment. He just opened the window and unbounded the girl. The girl immediately tried to open the door of the car and certainly failed. Again, the clout of vomit wanted to come out of her but she couldn't help herself other than suffocating. Nil offered a bottle of water. The girl could not take more than a sip. Now she vomited out of the half-open window as much as possible. Nil just tried to bundle her careless curls in his feast. Within a few minutes, the girl was senseless once again. Nil shouted again. 'Hari bhai! Stop the car, should I call Sir now? What will he say if the girl dies or something happens to her?'. Hari remained as indifferent as before. 'Where from you took her? Tell me! Tell me the truth, Hari. She doesn't even look like a bad girl. ' 'Who cares? Hari laughed at the sounds! Who cares if she is from a brothel or church!!'..' Church! Have you lost it? Is she really from a church?'...Hari replied after an unnecessarily prolonged silence 'Yes. she is. She is a girl from Kolhapur who came to the church to spend the rest of her life in medical work. Ha! Look at her fate! She is taken for what now.!' ' It is you, Hari, you are the demon who changed her life!!!'.'Fate!!! Food!. Have you seen fate?' 'Nil bhai! I never believed in fate. I believe in bread and life, as I did it for my bread. My hunger is my weakness and I am ready to do anything to please my hunger. "Nil took a handful of water and sprinkled it over the girl's face. The girl woke up again.' What is your name?" Mandira! the girl answered with a gust of sobbing. `` My life...my life had just started and they snatched me out of there"." Out of where? Nil shook her a little, I wanted to know everything. Out of where they took you out?" " From the Monastery. I used to stay in a girls 'hostel. I used to teach in a local orphanage of the Monastery in Patna.

...' My parents used to live there. But they killed them and put me in the orphanage. I studied Ayurveda there. I had my clinic. They broke it and threw me in the road. Then they took me to the farmhouse. I managed to escape and somehow got a job in the orphanage school."Ahh, God! Again, those monsters kidnapped me and brought me here." Mandira just broke down and was feeling tired. Nil asked in a firm voice 'Do you have any idea where you are right now?' 'No! ' Mandira's voice was helpless. This time Hari became adamant 'Hey! Nil bhai! No more, huh? enough is enough. Now don't force me to throw both of you out of the car. And Nil bhai, you stay out of these. Right?". Nil had a thought to call Kushan Sir but he lost

his mind. The car was on the way to Matheran. It was on the turn of a hairpin bend from Panvel high road.The car stopped in a remote village near Muldunge. Generally, in these routes, motor vehicles don't come but the people of Kushan Kanti can reach out to any bars. Hari stopped the car, came out of the and forced Mandira to take her baggage. Nil was going to protest but Hari didn't bother. The house was looking like an old homestay. The house lady was looking like a middle-aged ugly duckling. She looked around Mandira with a doubtful look and took her inside. Nil tried to look behind as much as possible but the old green wooden door was closed. The climate was pleasant and he had started to sweat like anything. He loosened his body on the plumpy seat cover of the car but couldn't relax himself. Hari came back till then and started the engine. They had to return to Mumbai that night. Work was pending there! A lot of work.

When Nil was a young boy, he learned to draw from a local artist. The artist had an exhibitor painting shop in the Government Museum of Art and Architecture. He taught Nil after the pencil sketch how slowly the shades of colors are poured inside. Then how the strokes go from thinner to deeper. When Nil was a teenager he tried his best to stroke the shapes and shades. In Kerala, the monsoon was like wild approaching Green Heaven. Everywhere the silver drops of rain had embraced the faded white clouds. The mist of vapor had wrapped the blanket of an unusual cold. One morning in front of his house lawn, he found a bunch of fresh lotus. It was half-bloomed, misty, and smelling wild. Later he came to know her mother had to supply it as an order. Nil placed one of them in a clay pot. He poured the bottle of blue into the pot of water. The water became blue. The pink and magenta shades of the lotus were swirling around the water. Some drops of rain drenched into it but it was not enough. Something was missing!!! Nil ran to the nearby pond, picked a handful of moss, and mixed it in the tub. The water was not crystal clear anymore but the lotus became vibrant., like a pious light amidst a mysterious night. Nil created a portrait out of his imagination and kept it in the corner of her study table. After a long year in Mumbai when Kushan Sir called him at midnight and offered a lump sum amount to hide a dead body in the outskirt jungle, Nil observed blood on the sack of the body. It was some colour that he had never seen to his artist uncle. He realized he was turning into the mysterious sky in his portrait and going far behind the usual colors of his life.

Nil sat in the coach again. Wrapped his blessings nicely and continued to read the Meghdutt once more ...." Tasya sthita, kathamapi pura, kautukadhan heto, ranta barspo, schira manucharo raja rajasya dadhau..."...King Kuber 's person that departed Yaksha observed towards those heart-melting clouds for prolonged hours and somehow controlled his tears. Looking towards the clouds a happy person also becomes absent-minded but one who is already delicate and departed out of a separation from his beloved never controls himself. At almost two o'clock Nil read it with a calm mind. Then he closed the book and went to bed. When he put off all the lights and plunged his body into the bed, the rain had already pushed up its speed. That night he had a dream of Mandira. As he had seen her on the lawn of the Matheran house. She was wearing a faded white salwar kameez, her eyes were dark but magnificent. Her braided hair was curling like a playful water snake. She was tall, thin, and intelligent. She was drying her clothes on the branches of the tree and became quite alert seeing Nil over the place. Nil stretched his hands as he wanted her to pay attention to something but a single word didn't come out of her voice. When he woke up it was almost eight. The day was cloudy but not shabby. It was not raining. He opened his diary to check the track of the day. Suddenly his phone rang. It was Hari. Hari told him to go to Matheran. He needed to deliver to the same house lady where they had dropped Mrinal last evening. Nil's eyes gleamed with some unknown sheer joy. He put on his best outfit, combed his hair with all filmy styles, and bathed with the perfume. In almost two hours he reached. The house looked a little less shabby than last night. The lawn in front looks quite green but no flowery plant he observed. Nil knocked on the door. The fat old lady opened it without any household courtesy, directly she asked in a harsh husky voice" Where is the order?"...Nil handed it over and started to look inside with a little curiosity. The old fat lady premonished something and closed the door in front. Nil felt angry and awkward. He hardly asked for the payment. He stepped outside and onto a big piece of stone. He lit up a cigarette and looked down the hill. Though it's approaching a monsoon still the surroundings look bright. Down by the way a few sturdy logs were engraved. There a few strings were hung where local women were putting their washed clothes. Suddenly Nil observed Mandira. She was wearing a pale blue but bright cotton saree. Her curly hair looked more curled in the daylight. The up-and-down movement of her hands around the strings and washing clothes reminded him of some Mohiniattam dance form he used to visit in his childhood. Mrinal looked pale but graceful from top to bottom. Nil threw his cigarette and ran down to her. "HI! Hello...did you recognize me? Yesterday? Yesterday I gave you water in the car...!!". Mrinal looked back and smiled. "Oh...you, so you came to visit my mother-in-law...right?". 'Mother-in-law!!!' Nil stepped backward a little...' your mother-in-law! Are you married?". Mrinal smiled again. Till the time she had finished, clothes were hanging around. ' Come! Let's sit there'. Both of them went a little further down to the river and sat. "I got married when I was nineteen. Before a few months, your people killed my parents as my father hid some gold from them. I used to run my own Ayurveda clinic at that time. They broke it. I became penniless, with nothing to leave with. One of my neighbors took all the interest in getting me married to Gagan. After a few months of my marriage, I came to know Gagan and his family are involved in drug supply. Maybe some other business too. Two times they tried to sell me out but every time I ran away. Your people bought me once before. So, they never stopped to follow me. They are the regular customers of my mother-in-law to purchase drugs. She only dragged my father-in-law and Gagan in this field. " Ohh! How was your husband then?" He was nothing but a puppet in their hand. The marriage was just a farce. Your team wanted to sell me out. I ran away. So again, they brought me back to my mother-in-law again." And what are you doing here now? Nil asked a callous question suddenly! Mandira laughed to her fullest and answered "Waiting for a new gutter!".

Slowly she started to move towards the house. Nil stood up but couldn't say anything. From the back line of her body, Mandira appeared to him as a floating cloud who lost her way and glided into an eternal void. Nil felt to call her again but something was stuck in his voice. What to say! Why to say? Mrinal faded away like a fringe of pale blue cloud. Nil returned within a couple of hours. Evening Hari came to meet and shouted 'Did you meet the girl today?' 'Which girl? Nil asked back. "Don't act! You know everything! Too much now. Why do you talk to her? And where is the payment?". Nil shrugged his shoulders and arrogantly answered 'That old lady is too much! She didn't even bother to ask for the payment. '....' Ahh bloody fool! It's not her you should ask for the payment. 'Hari shouted badly. 'Fine. I will go tomorrow and throw the money in your face!' Nil also raised his voice. After a prolonged heated argument, Hari left. That night Nil had a dream of some pale blue clouds. The clouds started to float from the northeast to the west and covered the golden glee of the summer. Morning around 7 am Nil woke up. It was a bright fair day. It was too early to wake up. Today's work had not been updated for him. He had still a few times. After a long time, he felt like taking out his paints and paintbrushes. He did so. The easel board was half broken and rescued from a long line of cobwebs. Nil took an old bedsheet and started to clean it. Once he was mid-way the rain speeded up. It was emitting dust from the air. His phone started to ring. It was Hari. He reminded him to collect the payment as early as possible. The old lady leaves the house around noon and goes for some work. Nil found it would take almost one and a half hours in the car if he started now and then. But he did not hurry. "Let it be at least 11.30 there!! I swear I will collect the payment and meet Mandira again ". The chosen one of his best, put half a bottle of his body spray, tried to look better than he is, and set off. Today the old lady gave him a rotten mossy smile and after a tough bargain gave the payment. Nil felt relieved and hid near a narrow lane. Around 12.15 pm he found the old lady coming out of the house and took the opposite way of the lane towards the station. He didn't even waste five minutes and turned up in front of the house. He knocked on the door but no one responded. 'Did Mrinal leave the place? Did she run again? 'Thoughts pondered over his thoughts. He looked back and forth and came back to his car with a gust of despair. When the car came down the narrow and wide lanes Nil could see Mandira in the front mirror. She was just passing the waterfall carefully. Her saree was tucked up to her thin fair knees. The waterfall lane was not full and fluffy but it was mossy and slippery. Mandira was looking bright today. Nil came back almost half a kilometre and honked. Mrinal slipped and sat on the stone itself. "What's going on? Why are you honking here?" Mrinal looked surprised! Nil took the car almost near Mandira and stopped the engine. "Why? Honking is not allowed in this route? My car, my wish!! Nil answered breathlessly with a gust of whimsical happy note in his voice. Mandira chuckled a little but didn't say anything. "Did you get your payment?" She asked now. Nil felt a little embarrassed "how do you know?". Mandira laughed at him. "Hà! My mother-in-law was planning yesterday not to give it to you." "Then she must have had to give her life ...Nil took the gun out of his back. Mandira looked at him but she was not scared. "How old are you? Why did you choose all the wrong ways? "She asked firmly looking at his eyes. Nil threw the gun on his back seat. Indifferently he answered, " I didn't choose anything, rather this way chose me". Mandira handed over a pile of some plants to Nil and said in a comical voice" Well! Now get me out of this way! I came to collect herbs for some medicines. Can you please take me home back? I am feeling tired!". Both of them got into the car. Mandira was wearing a mossy green saree. While taking an u turn Mandira slipped into him. Nil somehow controlled the speed of the car. It was about to cause an accident but they were saved. Nil stopped the car in front of that old wooden door. Mandira called him for a cup of coffee. Nil neither said no nor yes. He just followed Mandira upstairs. Mandira piled all the herbs in the corner of her room and turned on the switch of the electric kettle. "You make nice coffee. "Nil replied in some sober manners. "I have been a coffee lover since I was in Kerala. Did you ever have a sip of filter coffee? It is strong and delicious. " " I know. Once I was pursuing Ayurveda, I visited Kerala. There was a plethora of herbs! "Mandira's face suddenly looked very bright, remembering the bright days of the past. "Would you like to visit once more? Nil asked her with a child-like happy tune in his voice." It is my hometown there. ` Will you come there with me?' It was then Mandira's turn to laugh. ``...And what about your boss? Ha...ha...what do you think? will he book the tickets for us to say goodbye?". Nil couldn't say anything. Suddenly his phone rang " New stock came...come back soon'. `It will take the whole night to understand the accounts. ". Nil took a leave from Mandia and set out for Mumbai. Now in the middle of the day, it will take more than two hours to reach. Nil reached around 4 pm and joined his team. Some illegal transactions had happened last night. Nil started to maintain the account as he had been doing it for the last fifteen years. When he indulges in the settlement of such accounts all the colours of his palette start to swirl around him. First, it turns into a rainbow then it churns and churns and turns into a grey vibe. Today he could not concentrate on all these. Time and again the faded abstract lotus was creating a shape in front of his eyes." The lotus woman.... who is tall, darkly bright, full eyed and heavy breast, the deep naval, the trivanga waist, the tender toe, and the fluttery neck"...."The lines were taking a shape and gradually it turned Mandira". Nil stood up from the table and washed his face nicely. Who knows if all is happening out of bloody stress? It is true that his body and mind didn't receive any sexual comfort for the last six months but is it all about sex? The work took midnight to be completed. All of his teammates slept there only but Nil couldn't sleep. He was feeling tired, very tired. He sat in the hall with a small peg and started to play his broken mouth organ in a half-hearted tune, suddenly the loud honk of a white sedan awakened his mates too. A lanky tall middle-aged man entered. He is coming directly from Kushan Sir. There are two dead bodies in the car, they murdered yesterday night. He wanted them to hide it in the jungle nearby. Nil was not even feeling to stand. But Hari gave him an elbow stroke. They loaded the two bodies in their Zip and started towards Matheran. When the lanky man started from their place by mistake, he stepped into Nil's mouth Organ and kicked it off. Hari was driving as usual. Nil slept out of tiredness. When they reached the jungle side, it almost touched the fringe line of hibiscus red in the sky. They buried the two bodies in the jungle very quickly, the blood coming out of the body was looking clotted and fading till the time. The hissing tension of the night suddenly started to fall into a release when they two came out of the jungle. Hari went inside the car and in a minute fell into a deep sleep. Nil started to enjoy the beautiful dawn around the jungle side. Slowly the sky sprinkled from red to orange from every nook and corner. The dew drops fell on the tip of the leaf and suddenly turned on the diamond lights glittering the lash green. The daily workers started to be visible one or two. Nil was looking for some tea...."Tatra byaktang ,drishadi charana,nyasa ma ardhendu moule,...shashwat siddhai rupachita baling..bhakti namra pariya....Wherever on the stone you can see the footprints of the Lord Shiva, you must know that Yogis are constantly worshipping there. You also bow down to the footsteps so that you can get out of all the sins and seek moksha under the feet of Lord Shiva as a devotee...." who was that? A great sound chanting mantras and elaborating wisely was coming out nearly. Nil was charmed and started to find the voice. Nil followed the voice like an enchanted one. He found a hut thatched of leaves. Out of the hut, some smoky swirl was flying here and there. The wooden door was quite open. Nil entered without knocking. "What a celestial atmosphere appeared in front of him! An old but robust man was chanting some Sanskrit Slokas. He was sitting on a wooden couch and Mandira was sitting at his feet repeating the same. Both of their voices were creating a floating harmony vibrating the hilly Valley. The crimson sun had arrived at its fullest and welcomed the morning rituals. Mrinal stood up suddenly 'You! Here...at this moment!'. The old man looked at the woman's face and went inside the room. Nil felt more than hesitant as just right there he had committed a crime. "I was just passing by...I didn't want to stop you. I mean ...you are...". The old man came out of the room again. " Child! I am the Sanskrit Guru of the local School. We were chanting some slokas from Meghdutt. ...Any idea, what is it?". Nil stood up blank and perplexed. Mandira took up a heavy book from a wooden bookshelf and handed it over to Nil. "Here you go, read it sometimes ". Nil smiled, begged a sorry from both of them, and came back to his car. He dumped the heavy book on the back seat of his car and started the car. When he came back to his place, he discovered his mouth organ was lying down on the floor smashed and crashed. Nil went back to his flat by the afternoon itself and he was feeling lonely, really lonely. Around evening he realised he had a high fever. The fever was increasing quite high. Nil called the doctor but the doctor was out of station. The last option Nil called Mrinal. He was aware of his Ayurveda knowledge. Mandira reached almost at night. Nil was feeling so weak that he couldn't even think how Mrinal managed to reach him. When Mandira reached Nil was shivering out of fever. Within a fraction, she covered himself with the blanket lying on the floor. She was already carrying some medicines which she fed Nil. She took Nil in her arms and slowly put her head on the pillow. Nil loved the warmth and unconsciously tightened Mandira as much as possible. Nil's shivering transmitted to Mandira. She also shivered in the uttered warmth of a man after a long year. The medicine worked and Nil slept. Beside him, Mandira also slept wrapping the same blanket. She was feeling tired from the journey. Early in the morning, Mandira woke up. Nil's fever still reduced but still he was sleeping. She kept her right hand on his forehead. It was all normal temperature. She felt relieved. She went to the kitchen which was too unfamiliar to find anything. Mandira somehow managed to prepare coffee and came to Nil's balcony. Her sleep was not complete. The height of the balcony was a little low and Cozy. It was good to see from there. Hardly two or three sips are done, suddenly she found a warm existence at her back trying to wrap herself inside him. Yes, it was very much of Nil. Mandira couldn't even get sometimes to be surprised before Nil's both strong robust hands locked her and his lips started to suck Mandira's. Mandira just melted in the warmth of the touch. Neither she thought nor she wanted to. It was just a flow both swept away clinching together. The bed, the blanket, the pillows still emitted the fever of last night. But those two passionate pressed and scratched and bitten all the fever. Mrinal wanted to tell something in between but Nil didn't want to listen so it had already crossed the day to listen and unlisten. So around late afternoon Mrinal returned home. Nil was not feeling like working for the day so he also took a break. For another few hours, he was lost in his broken color palette. He tried to pick the colors and strike them in some shapeless shapes which he didn't know, didn't even want to know but He was trying to get involved, involved as much as possible. He was feeling weak, very weak as he could not give any stroke. The urge to create the unknown led him to the very known world of him and all the strokes created a crimson that he didn't want at all.

On the other hand, Mandira was quiet and didn't even think to call Nil. She kept herself very busy with work. Some pleasure and pain both were drenching out of her body and mind but it was not the time to get wet by monsoon. A few, actually a lot of work was pending. She had miles to go before she slept, she wanted to rebuild her clinic again. She knew very well her mother-in-law was planning to sell her, but still, she wanted to carry on from there only. At Least the repose, she got there, the bread and butter…who else will provide the same? When her parents were killed, her clinic was smashed, she starved for two days and still the trauma led her to a nightmare. She doesn't know Nil. What if he also tries to sell him. Today he made love to her but is there any assurance that tomorrow he won't mislead her in some more new path. Life has become treacherous to her. She has fallen through the thorns and bleeds everywhere. Mrinal was standing alone as she wanted to. Each and every touch of Nil was putting a mug of fire from her top to toe. She could feel how much desired touch it was to her. When she used to get a touch from her husband, she was young and all these were very much routine to her. Like a day-to-day story but today when Nil touched her it was different, it was like someone filled his feast with a handful of dust color and sprinkled throughout her every part of body, mind, and soul. Mrinal felt a sunrise around her. Dawn of soft, bright light around her navel cluttered through the smoky lines of some mysterious lights and touched the fringe line of the sky.

Nil was not fully cured of fever. Still, it was on and off but he was in his full senses. During the whole day, he tried to call Mandira several times but it didn't get picked. By the evening Nil became impatient and started his car towards Mrinal's place. He just got to know why Mrinal was so silent. Is that their intimacy that was bothering her or something else? When Nil reached, the sun had already set leaving some orange lines towards the horizon line of the meadow. He found Mrinal crushing something sitting on a solid rock. A dim lantern was lying straight at her feet. Her sari was a bit reluctant to manage the tidy dignity like the other days. Nil took the back side of the road, parked his car down the bush, and silently stood behind her. Mrinal saw the shadow but didn't expect anyone around her at this time. She turned around and saw Nil was looking at her completely dipped in passion. His eyes were reflecting the lights of hope and his lips were shivering to utter a lot. He just held Mandira hard and asked in a firm voice "Why didn't you pick up my phone? Why? "Mrinal was still and silent but she also didn't understand when she rounded her hands around Nil's waist unknowingly. Nil wanted to ask more and Mrinal wanted to remain silent for a longer time but when it was a blue glowing dark both of them didn't know when they stuck to each other like a magnet each other and both of their lips were just sucking, pressing and biting each bit of darkness. The stony meadow just felt their vibrating hearts in every moment of that evening and after a long-awaited summer, that night had shown a line of thunder in the dark deep sky. A drop, two drops of rain slowly turned into a heavy shower. Nil and Mandira rushed towards the broken temple of the village. The shade was not enough to protect both of them but they remained a united body, for a long time they turned, sometimes they twisted but exited with a full bloom of happiness. "Falling in love with me means risking yourself you know" Nil murmured suddenly. "Are you telling it to me or yourself? I never told you I had fallen in love with you. "Mandira tried to laugh a lot but every effort turned into a pale smile. Nil held her cheeks in his palms and raised them towards him. The faint light of the temple serine surpassed through her teary eyes. "Who told you don't love me? And how long will you try to stay away from me? "My life is not smooth, Nil..."The outbursts of thunder rounded the nook and corner of the temple". Nil and Mrinal seemed like two children of deep darkness amidst the whole atmosphere. "Do you think Kushan Kanti will allow me a normal life with you?" Do you think my mother-in-law will free me from you? The day before yesterday two people came to buy me again. Still, the bargaining is ongoing. Mrinal started to shiver like a drenched bird under the shade. Nil tried to give her all the warmth he saved till. Suddenly several thunders were falling hampering the whole peace of the temple area. Nil and Mandira were compelled to enter into the serine area for a better shelter. After the rain stopped the clouds started to clot and close. Mrinal found herself tight in the arms of Nil. Both of them were unaware that the day was a full moon. The moon was trying to come out of the clouds just like a newborn baby out of the womb crimson but aware of its existence. Nil whispered in the ear of Mandira" I deserve a new life". Mrinal kept her right palm on the chest of Nil and replied " You are meant to be". Suddenly Nil took out the gun from his left-sided back pocket and kept it on the shrine of the temple. The lamp was still reflecting some defusing dim light and, in the light, the gun looked like a big emancipated crow. Nil continued to say "Mandira, I got an offer for painting from a Craft Company in Kerala. I will be leaving next month." Mrinal took Nil's hand in hers and pressed softly along with the gentle strokes of her fingers "Can I join you, Nil? I will open my own Ayurveda clinic again there. Both of them looked into each other and remained silent. The silence lasted like the law of the lamp for long. Nil came back to his place. After dropping Mrinal in at her place. Just as both of them didn't observe two black shadows followed them from the beginning to the end of this sudden monsoon.

The next morning Nil posted a letter in detail to Kushan Kanti that he was not going to continue here anymore. Nil started to pack his leftover things from here and there. Though he didn't have many. Suddenly he discovered the 'Meghdutt ' in his bag pack. Maybe Mandira had kept it inside by mistake. Nil touched the cover page of the book from top to bottom, left a few gentle strokes on it, and decided to read the book in some free time. Tied up with all the leftovers he called Mandira. Her phone rang twice, thrice and more but she didn't pick up. Nil couldn't hold his patience till evening. He took his car and came to Mrinal's place but the old house was not even lit up with a single candle. It was a fearsome dark around the house. Nil couldn't decide with his brain for some time. He stood perplexed. "Is it that they took Mrinal? Is that they sold her again? Then what is it? With every single doubt in mind, He looked at the sky. He didn't know if Almighty had understood his speechless emotion or not but the time and again roaring of thunder chasmed his whole heart. With a gust of despair, when Nil came back home, he found Hari sitting at his doorstep. He gave a top-to-bottom look towards Nil, the look was cold, heinous. Nil hated it. Within a moment with the bad rows of yellow spotted teeth, he gave a big smile which was not enough for a smile rather a joke seemed to be cracked on Nil. "Brother we are going to Matheran today only. Kushan Sir told. You wrote a letter to him

So, he gave you a new place. We are going now only. Finishing up to this he again gave the same smile. Within a moment every scenario became clear to him. He held the collar of Hari and shouted "Where is Mrinal?... Tell me where is Mrinal? Did you sell her? Around night they both set out for Matheran. Kushan Kanti had rejected his letter and posted him there for one year. For one year Nil had to work from the same location. No leave will be approved for outstation. Kushan Kanti's people are off to bring his mother here. Nil felt like kicking the world. One year now he can't even spend without Mrinal. What his mother will think when she comes to know about his profession? That interior Company will never offer a job to him. All the colors started to swirl around his eyes and turned black. Above all, Nil started to like the small single room, a small kitchen, and a cozy balcony at least provided a little sense of privacy. Of course, Hari is the full-time doorkeeper and comrade in all his work. Still night time when Hari sleeps Nil sits on the couch with his cup of coffee and tries to read the Meghdutt though he doesn't understand most of the meanings of Sanskrit. Nil smiles at his mind. If Mandira was here, she could have explained meaning to meanings. but where is Mrinal?' Almost three months ago he didn't even receive any news of her. Mrinal roams around in his dream like a pale pink lotus and melts away in a cast of dawn light. 'Where are you, Mandira? Are you still alive?'. Kushan Kanti has given you a new number. The old one Hari is using. Sometimes Nil feels like killing Hari but he is an artist. He loves to create and he does know how to destroy. He didn't even commit a single murder whatever he did was bury the bodies and that was also his bread and butter. Only God knows and Mandira knows how much he hates this life.

Mandira found herself awake in a kind of godown. All around her were antique curios. She felt slightly feverish and had too much body pain. A slight slender bloodline was coming out of her forehead and a deep source of pain. She tried to protect herself as much as possible but she couldn't. She failed to call Nil before they snatched her phone and smashed it. Mandira was running like a wounded deer and tried to save her but they hit her head and there was a blackout. Within half an hour she realized that a huge piece of physics had entered the room. She could see only the shadow of his backside. Mandira was trembling inside. Suddenly the shadow turned into Kushan Kanti. The heartless, ruthless Kushan Kanti snatched her parents, destroyed her home, and finished her clinic. Thousands of thunders busted in her heart. She tried to shout but God only knows who has sprinkled sand in her mouth. She closed her eyes with all of her sheer fear. "Nil, where are you?" Mandira's eyes were over flooded with tears. Kushan sounded like a wounded cheetah. "What did you think? You will run away from me? You are mine. You are born to be mine. You don't have any escape from me." He sat on the chair in front of her. The cheetah finally grabbed his prey under her claws. His eyes were reflecting the glimpses of greed. Mandira sank into her soundless sobs. Her cry reached the sky.

It was the fourth day Nil learned to read Meghaduta slowly. He was stuck in words but shifted to the emotions. His mind was finally settled. His heart was sad still he could feel Mandira in every sound of Mandira. The clouds took the shape of fluttering birds and flew away from his cozy balcony. Do they go to Mandira? Do they carry his message to her? Nil stands on the balcony with a cup of coffee. He thinks of the dreams they saw together. It was the twentieth day Mandira took place in Kushan's private beach resort. This place is too sunny. Mandira looked at the sky for some shades of clouds but there were not any. Mandira used to close her eyes, press her lips, and pray to God daily. She was placed in the private beach resort of Kushan Kanti and given some work of housekeeping. Kushan's people keep an eye on her strictly. That day

Kushan went but he said he would be back soon. Till the time Mandira is awake and alert. She knows that the next time when Kushan Kanti comes will not be spared. Mrinal counted the days like a prisoned bird in a cage fluttering her wings, sometimes like a rebel, sometimes tucking her wings, closed her eyes, and used to sit like a fatigued bird. The sparkling bright eyes turned into dark circles. Her tiny little naughtiness turned into dull shabby monotony. Her dreams of cultivating Ayurveda left her on the wrong track. She lost all her interest in her life. God only knows what Kushan is going to do with Mandra! Are they going to keep her herbs? Are they going to sell her? What is next Oh God. Mandira feels like pulling her hair in despair.

The next evening Nil was returning from his work and suddenly he saw Megh on the junction of the road talking to someone. Megh Mallar Chatterjee once used to be Kushal's partner upon a time. That time Nil was very young. They fought over some money issues and fell apart. But being in the underworld also he was a kind-hearted person. Megh knew that Nil loved to paint. So, he used to give him art materials so many times. Nil used to be very happy to see all those staff. Nil took the turn and reached Megh within a second. He horned from the back. Megh looked back. He couldn't identify Nil. "Hattima Tim Tim Tara mathe pare dim."Nil started to recite the old Bengali rhyme Megh used to recite. Suddenly there was a sparkle in his eyes. Megh stretched his arms with sheer joy at recognizing Nil. Ultimately both of them sat in a coffee shop and tried to unfold themselves as much as possible. Nil Megh had started his own business of import and export. No more he continued the underworld. He paid the penalty for his past deeds and started a new life. Nil was just feeling the fellowship of their old times. Still, he was so comfortable with Megh. Nil started a prolonged discussion of his growth with Kushan. Gradually he raised the topic of Mrinal and asked if he could help him but Megh didn't have any idea of Mrinal. Megh was looking for accommodation as he got some work in the place but he was unable to manage any. All the hotels of the Matheran also were booked. Nil took Megh with him. When both of them entered Hari looked disgracefully to them but Hari used to like Megh a lot before. Nil knew that Hari would not have complained about Megh. Moreover, it was just a one-night stay. Somehow three of them enjoyed the whole evening eating and chatting. Night around 11 pm Hari went to sleep. Megh and Nil sat together. Megh advised Nil to talk to Kantak. Kantak was the culprit who used to buy women from Kushan. Megh gave Kantak 's number to Nil. Both of them called and within an hour the picture came in front of Nil where they might have kept Mandira. Kantak was unwilling to provide all those secrets to Nil but Megh pressured him with a large amount of money and the greedy Kantak couldn't control. "The private beach was not that safe for Mandira. Anytime they could have sold her out. Mandira might be spending her days in an ordeal. Kushan might have tortured her a lot. All those thoughts encroached in his mind relentlessly. Nil couldn't focus on anything. Only the thoughts of Mandira crowded his heart cloud heavy. The words from Meghaduta were about to float in front of her eyes. The color palette used to create different shapes, sizes, and fringes of Mandira. Nil used to think, get drunk, and be absorbed in the thoughts of Mandira. He couldn't get any remedy to rescue her. On the other hand, Mandira used to spend his days alone, on an amorous, lonesome beach. Morning to night she tried to keep herself busy with household work. She knew their plans to sell her. Many times she was forced to send them to Kushan's bed. Every Time she threatened them by keeping a dagger in her neck that she would finish himself. Those people were clever enough to understand that once she hurt herself, they would be unable to sell her. They were waiting for a big party that would offer a lump sum for Mandira. Megh wanted to help. He used to call Nil regularly but he was helpless. Almost one year has passed like this. Mandira became a permanent staff of Beach Resort. She was an efficient worker. Kushan changed his mind not to sell her. Maybe he expected Mandira would have changed her mind. Nil does not go for any field operation. Hari only handled everything. Most of the time nowadays he takes care of accounts only and the whole room is getting full of his paintings. The racks, every nook, and corner are visible with the colors. Meghdutt lied to the coach silently. The words used to give a call to him every day but Nil deliberately tried to avoid them. He knew that where

Mandira was stucked the try of protecting her would be in vain. Mandira was getting lost in a labyrinth. Each circle used to create a different shade in Nil's mind but it used to vanish at the end. He couldn't even bring them in a shape or size. Is Mandira fading away from his life? All the best Nil could have prayed for a deep, deep sleep. A great sleep only could have supported him in a little restoration of peace. On the other side, Mandira was getting settled with her working life. Somehow the customers of the beach resort liked his service very much. She used to be cool, calm, and soothing with everyone. People used to like her company a lot. Kushan and his people observed everything and decided to keep her there only. Mandira was falling sick day by day. She had developed several infections and weaknesses.

Nil on the other hand couldn't come to the beach resort. Though he tried several times. Megh personally tried to help her several times but he failed after a certain time. He was helpless. One year had passed like this. Nil ran away from Matheran and went back to Kerala. His mother took her last breath at Kushan's place.

After his mother had passed away, he didn't have any compulsion to continue Kushan's service nor did he want money anymore. He just wanted to go back and live a simple lifestyle. In Kerala, he found a sort of mental peace. He repaired his old house and started painting classes at home for small children. Several times he had contacted the interior Company but no response as usual. Nil never used to be frustrated. Rather he was feeling happy as an artist. He completed reading Meghaduta during the course and amidst the heavy rainfall of Kerala. He had a complete solitude. He didn't even have anyone to interrupt or disturb him. In Front of his small house, there was a four-acre land of lush green paddy field. Every day the fresh flowing water of rain used to nourish the growing rice and Nil used to nourish his mind as Mandira used to. Recently he had spoken to two young boys who were learning Ayurveda in Kerala. Nil offered them a room in his old house if they wanted to open their clinic. The two boys almost agreed. Nil was also finding peace among all those. One morning he wanted to visit the northern side of their land where the river was flowing utmost. It was very early morning. Nil had just finished his morning chants and reached the river bank. He was mesmerized by the floating clouds, mists, and lush green of the surroundings and suddenly he heard a loud honk at his backside road. "So early in the morning! "He was surprised. Generally, no cars go from this route at this time. He looked back. It was Megh. He looked like that he had just crossed the bar of something horrible and turned up in front of Nil. Nil silently appeared in front of him" What's the matter? Is everything fine?" Megh held both hands of Nil, looked into his eyes, and said "Mandira is no more. Last week she passed away in Alibaug Resort only with a sudden increased fever and cardiac failure. Nil closed his eyes. He remembered the pale soft blue saree of Mrinal which she had worn at first day they met and those bright eyes that he looked into several times during their lovemaking. Further, he could feel his colour palette started to swirl around and produce soft fluffy fluid clouds floating toward the grey sky. A drop of two drops of tears had started to come out of his eyes.

THE END

THE NIGHT: MOMENTS CREATES ITS CAST

Manisha never thought it could have happened. It was not meant to be. Whatever had happened last night, Manisha never thought it would happen in her life. From her childhood, she was soft by nature. She wanted to cling over the world but the world always walked away from her. When the buds were about to bloom in her garden, she used to assume the colours of the flowers were upcoming. She used to develop attachments with every plant, flower, leaf, and insect in every nook and corner of the garden. The gardener used to pour water during the day and just after reaching school, she used to sit and observe everything. 'Dada.... What do the centipedes eat? Rice? Butter?' 'The gardener used to laugh a louder. He used to laugh and laugh at the nuisance questions of the little girl but Manisha used to create her world of colours, essence and creatures. Manisha was extremely happy within the imaginary world. One day she stepped into adolescence. The flower's petals turned into a single lotus blossom inside her and that is the yearning of the sense, sensory and sensuousness. The whole body and mind of Manisha turned itself into a garden. The conflict was not the childhood. The conflict was the adolescence when Manisha started to be alienated from each one. People say near and dear but

Manisha still could not find any near and dear. She searched and searched and found too but they just looked at Manisha's bodily bloom, they did not even look at Manisha's heart and soul. Manisha's soul started to reflect colors. Manisha was very much aware of it. Still even in midnight when the Mogra vine smelled the airy skyline Manisha used to feel lonely. Her body, and mind wanted to clutch someone whose touch would heal her but she didn't find any. Time and again the garden grew young and green. The saplings turned into groves and the gardener passed away long back Manisha felt alone again. At this age, her playmates indulged in all types of frivolous hullaballoos but Manisha didn't even feel any interest. She had started to make shells around her. Her parents never came close to her. They just wanted to get rid of their responsibility. They didn't even let her peruse any of her choices, hardly she was allowed to have any. She didn't get a high-salaried job, she couldn't manage a high-profile boyfriend. Her parents were ambitious. They could not even understand the consequence of an unequal social marital status. Manisha got married to the son of some great personality and reached the dignity of some false identity. The cage remained cage only. Every status of Manisha became expensive only except her soul. Her soul started to be fatigued and unwatered. Her parents were extremely happy with the social upliftment but Manisha started to lose all the petals of her garden. During that time, she gave birth to two sons. Round the routine and responsibility, the fringe line of her hair grew silvery and she had lost the strength of her wings hardly she ever had any. She found herself losing the track in its way different. She found herself, she recognised herself, she valued herself, and she humiliated herself. Sometimes she killed herself. At the very moment from her deep sleep, she heard the call of the petals. they were asking her to water themselves. Manisha woke up. She decided to make a world of her own. Her very own but the bird who never flew before how she will fly at every step, she confronted lack of confidence. After a certain period, Manisha got married to a rich person. That time Manisha became partially happy because she conceived and perceived the fake happiness followed by a marriage. Till she was unaware of the status of her imprisonment. She was not confident enough about her personality, but now she started to face the list of barriers and a perfect identity crash. She stumbled over the unrelaxing zone of a lifeline. Especially the nights seemed to appear as a nightmare to her every time. The guy she got married had only money, neither physical health nor high-spirited mental health. His purpose in life reminded Manisha of a pig. His snoring, his firing, his unconventional way of speaking and throwing bad jokes all swirled around the tummy of Manisha, like a clit of vomiting which she neither shallow nor spit out. Manisha started to swirl around her world and tried to find some absolute purpose in her life. Suddenly she realized she was just behaving in front of many unknown people. She accepts her split personality, rather she tries to call it a broken personality. The rich fat man gobbled her original personality into a behaved, mannered, and trimmed way and cascaded off her spontaneous being tucked into the shell like a tortoise. The day somehow, she managed to work in an NGO but at night it was all boring to her. The sex life was dry and dull, as she never felt sensuous or jolly excitement out of it. It was just a daily mechanism out of a sheer sense of dissevered times she went to her parents to spend a few days but the days were not peaceful, as those guys didn't understand her marital discord, and she could not open up to them, she did not even feel a bridge within them to communicate. A strong silence had started to eat Manisha slowly and silently. Her household used to make a strong voice and noise every day inside her heart but she was feeling empty from the core of her heart. She could hear a strong hollow sound that was terrific and dragging her towards the high altitude of loneliness. The trimmed and changed personality had started to reflect as the things started to appear around her, it was different, and it was difficult. As her husband's family was quite rich, Manisha never had to struggle with money but struggled with her mental state every time, every minute. Moreover, she carried a baby that plunged her into the dark, deep, density of depression. She was standing at the turning point of her life. Manisha tried to swim and swim out of it but the more she wanted to float, the more she slipped into. Once her baby was born, she started to nurse the baby boy, almost every night she used to have a nightmare she was walking on the top of a wall which was mossy and messy, and after a few steps, she just fell from an unmeasurable deep height that was leading her to a dark long way. slowly and gradually, she lost all of her interest in the flow of life. Her life overflowed under the world of misconception, depression, misunderstanding and mismatch. She became a desert completely during the day and night. Once on a rainy day, Manisha was home alone, and even the baby boy also went for a Puja with the other family members. Manisha was putting water into the saplings from the water pots. She had placed all the saplings around her balcony. The droplets were drenching out of the creepers from the beam of the balcony. In the afternoon, she got busy with her NGO work. Around the evening, she received a link from her friend group and found a few of her favourite dishes in the restaurant newly opened Sanjivani, the rising rejuvenation. Manisha did not take much time and quickly ordered a few of her favourite dishes online. Manisha was home alone bored but happy enough to enjoy her freedom and was feeling free spirit for that day. She felt like during the whole day, she lived her own life happily, she could do at least whatever she wanted to do. Around eight forty-five at night, her order arrived. The delivery boy was extremely courteous and spontaneous. After delivering he just chuckled and said 'Thank you mam ordering from us! you have a good choice of food'. Manisha observed the guy was not even talking like a simple delivery boy.

Rather he was more handsome than the others and talked also very politely. From the corner of her viewpoint, Manisha was feeling to talk to him more for a while as she was feeling an urge from the inside of her heart. The guy was just turning back when he stumbled on the shoe rack and pressed his finger on the broken part of the shelf due to a cut on his finger. The cut was extremely small but Manisha found enough reason to call him inside the house' You can come inside for first aid! Manisha called him soberly. 'I am fine, it is nothing but a scratch', the guy tried to be as normal as before but Manisha insisted. The guy entered the house. Manisha was wearing a black gown. She was not an unusual beauty but she had something in her that the guy found extremely unusual. `By the way, I am Abhimanyu. I run the small restaurant, Sanjeevani.'Manisha handed him a small piece of cotton with a pinch of Dettol and a band-aid with a completely open eye on him. 'So, are you the owner? not the delivery guy, right? 'Oh! Certainly not! but I don't mind being the delivery guy if my customer is so beautiful like you. 'Manisha just smiled but she was feeling a sense of happiness inside her. Abhimanyu was tall, dusk and a bit careless but all these added enough to Manisha. The band-aid slipped on the floor and Manisha just managed to pick it up and press it on the thumb of Abhimanyu. They were not even at a distance of an inch, Manisha was just about to listen to her heartbeat, Abhimanyu just took her lip inside the deep of him and started to suck it. Manisha felt the cloud break into the room and flood them away with a heavy shower. Another few hours later, they just broke into each other. They could not count the fractions of seconds, minutes and hours. They were just floating by the tide of passion. Together they were creating the chemistry of the night. Around the early morning, Abhimanyu left. Manisha was still in deep sleep. She never finds herself so relaxed as before. She was just looking like a girl floating in a lotus petal. Around 8 am, she woke up. Her family came back meanwhile. Manisha took a bath, tried to look fresh as much as possible, and came back to the household. All of a sudden there was a vibration in her phone…` keep on missing Sanjivani. So, what's next?'

THE END

THE UNKNOWN TERRACE: JOURNEY TOWARDS UNEXPLORED

The security guard was shouting from a long back. The balcony was too small to look around. Still, Titli could see the saplings of Mogra from the outage. was desperate to find Krishna. Inside the single accommodation house, a small pressure cooker was peeping through the planes of three parted windows. The outside couch of the half garden and half balcony was brief and tidy just as Krishna likes. The first time Titli entered the house she fell in love with the house Just as she fell in love with Krishna at first sight. Titli knew never in this life Krishna would have understood her feelings still she fell in love with Krishna. She never wanted to marry him or have any social relationship with him. She just wanted to love him. When she used to take him, every part of her body cried for him. A cry from the deep of his soul. Krishna was never bothered by all these. He regularly kept on indulging from one girl to another many times he was rude to Titli because of her growing disgusting feelings. Titli agreed always it was always all about her. Krishna was very straightforward from the core of his heart, he just wanted to be physical with Titli, initially, Titli agreed with all of his conditions. Titli liked every moment with Krishna as she enjoyed her fullest with the pleasure of tears. As Krishna used to touch her, she started to explore herself but she understood Krishna was indulging in it just to seek the pleasure he was neither attached nor involved. Once their passion used to get over, Krishna used to leave the room and Titli was meant to be all alone. Many times, she told Krishna about her feelings. Krishna stopped her carelessly. He used to be irritated, He used to say the words of liking, the words of feelings should not be expressed time, and again, the taste turns bad otherwise. Titli was involved in his thoughts suddenly the flow came back by the sounds of the security guard 'Since last night bhaiya did not come back'." Madam. Why don't you call him? Titli did not know what to answer or how to answer. She used to meet Krishna very rarely. Sometimes just for a casual talk and sometimes to exchange with each other, which was very spontaneous. Krishna did not even utter a single word while Titli used to cry. Krishna used to be busy in his way. He was a painter and a born artist. He used to exhibit his decors and paintings for his commercial places. He was a commercial artist who used to utilize his talents tactfully. Titli but she could not stop herself from loving Krishna. Every nook and corner she used to search for Krishna. She knew very well that Krishna took all the fun out of her. All the means, Krishna was longing for was a physical pleasure. Titli was flooded away by everything. She knew that She was a mother, she was a wife but nothing could stop her. Krishna had that warmth, that passion in his every bit of attitude that was inevitable to her. Inevitable to resist, inevitable to protect, inevitable to stop. It was a flow indeed. When the call came, Titli could not believe Khrishna was missing. She was not even aware of Krishna's present update which Krishna hardly used to share with her. Krishna was a struggling and rising artist. He used to mingle with different types of people. He used to visit many places, many times, many times, he asked to join Titli but he didn't agree. Krishna wished for freedom, an unquestioned freedom for wings. An ever-blue sky to flutter, the sheer joy of life. He was younger than Titli but he didn't care. He wanted to be physical with her. So, he did.

He dreamt of seeing people, he dreamt of seeing countries. He loved to drink the lease of life; he did not care about other's feelings. Krishna hated the social barrios of life. He hated the narrow paths of living. All the way he wanted was freedom and emancipation. Titli saw her first time when she went to her studio. She was looking for a real painting. A painting where the color will be neither dark nor deep. She wanted the colors of the painting to float like clouds. She wanted to place it on her balcony side where all the plants were mounting the colors together. She just wanted to have a painting there. Vishakha told her about Krishna. Krishna was a painter by passion, and by profession. Titli immediately decided to visit her studio. Ayan remained too busy with his officiation and knew he would never spend a single minute in a studio with an unknown artist. Titli used to go there all alone. Vinod Vihari Road 36 by lane. The road was too narrow to take a cab. She left her cab there only. The driver was a bit rude in handling the narrow hazards. So, he asked for more fare, and Titli was in a bad mood. The House was looking like an old heritage. The first floor seemed to be occupied by some working women. The Scrap she was holding in her hand was written 2nd floor. So, she climbed the old stiff stairs. The 2nd floor was more than a garden. All the indoor and outdoor plants were placed so beautifully that a person who will enter immediately forget about the old broken look of the house. Towards the north straight end, the door was open. Outside of the door, a few bottles of colors, paintbrushes, and a few canvases were littered. Titli understood that was the room of Krishna. She pulled her saree a little bit, held her handbag tight, and knocked on the door from outside though the door was wide open and the artist was half visible from the outside sitting backside towards the door and putting a few strokes in his canvas. Krishna looked back at the knocking sound. He found the lady who was standing at his door was profound. The description might be a little difficult for others but an artist never sees, he visualizes always. Krishna visualized Titli from a different angle. The sky-blue saree was looking like a wave. Her Curley long hair appeared as a fallen cascade and her deep eyes looked liquid to him. In an overall appearance, Titli appeared a flowing river in front of him. He looked at her in a full eye." Yes Mam, what can I do for you? This was the first reply from him. Titli entered, sat, and looked at the beautiful paintings hanging around.

Sunlight was coming from both sides of open windows and made the colors brighter, and more vivid. ` I felt the room as a real one, it has life and it breathes as well'. Titli started to fly away from flower to flower at the age of thirty-eight, she could feel her soul full of sixteen. She stopped in front of a black horse whose manes were white, eyes were sparkling and body was tight and robust." I want the same. Can I buy it?" She asked with a hidden excitement in her eyes. "But that one is already sold mam" ...Krishna replied confidently. Krishna was bold and handsome. He was hardly twenty-six. A floral shirt with three open buttons, wavy brownish hair with all careless abandon, deep thick eyebrows, big eyelashes, floating eyesight. He was very attractive in his first appearance. Titli also looked at him in her full eyes." Lakh jug hiye hiye rakhlu,tabu hiya jurano na gelo".Titli lost her way in his eyesight on the very first day. This labyrinth is mind-made. Titli knew she would find the way out neither nor did she expect it. Once She got married to Ayan, she never looked at her. She wore all the bangles of customs one by one in her own hands and the skyline remained to be left narrower. Arjun their son is almost thirteen. Now Titli was slowly getting wings back, Colorless but still able to fly. Those wings of wishes only suddenly cherished the dreams of original painting collections. So, by the tide of time, Titli met Krishna. Long time they looked at each other. Titli asked "Can you paint one more for me? I want it for my home.""Hmm...I have to check my dates for other paintings and then will let you know.

Krishna replied a little careless and looked up with indifference. Titli was offended but still felt a little amused by this type of behavior took the wooden stool back from Essel and sat comfortably. She pulled her saree a little back and took the bottle in her hand where all the paint brushes were getting soaked. She squeezed the brushes from the clots of old colors and started to wipe them with saree pallu." What are you doing madam? Your saree with get spoilt". Krishna stretched her hand to take his brushes back. Titli returned with all care. Both of their fingers touched. Krishna's hands were as beautiful as the strokes of his brushes. "Okay, will make one more for you but are you sure to take the same one? I can paint a variety also for you." Oh! That will be nice of you! '. The choice is yours.Titli agreed. Krishna took out all of his catalogs and handed them over to Titli." can sit on the coach if you want". Titli observed that the building was old but Krishna had made his room quite stylish. On the wall, his paintings of different shapes and sizes are visible to be hung. On the floor a single mattress-sized coach. A light color bedspread and the white net curtain reflect the lights more and ahead. A few shelves are hanging around the wall corners and the creeper money plants are catching the beauty around. Four more indoor plants are kept around the four-floor corners as well. A few terracotta showpieces enhance the beauty of all the simplicity surrounding by. She looked around the room. The room smells some artistic purity, some extract of good feeling, and an overall look of ecstasy. Titli used to dream of a room like this when she was a teenager but man proposes and God disposes. She did not find any room for herself rather she became the home decor of someone's room. She got married to Ayan, Ayan was a completely work-oriented person. Then Arjun came and more years had passed like a tide of time. By the time Arjun grew Titli became stronger, and more mature. The fringe lines of her hair turned the grey color and her mind also turned grey from the rainbow horizontality remained a leftover of herself and clutched on her few leftover hobbies like painting, singing, a gardening. Arjun was about to emerge; Ayan was floating in the mid-ocean of his office and Titli found herself at the threshold of middle age. All of them went their way. Titli could not even find it. She used to be a painter when she was young. So Titli plunged herself into the world of colors. One morning Titli took out all of his colors and canvas out of the hidden chest of her cupboards. The colors were dried, and the canvas was broken. She tried to fix it but could not. One of her friends advised her to meet some painters and to visit some exhibitions so that she would have some ideas new to start fresh. Titli decided to carry on the first idea better she visited a few artists' corners and bought some new pictures. So, she concentrated a little more on her art gallery balcony where she used to spend her own corner time. Krishna was soft to her within a few seconds and assured her to draw a beautiful new one. He stretched his hands towards Titli for the brushes. Titli returned the remaining two but all of her eyes remained stuck in him. Krishna was hardly twenty-six, half-fair, tall, and beautiful. Krishna's eyes were bold, big eyelashes and a glowing body. A soft glow of health was coming out of his whole body and it reflected some reflections. Titli remained lost in him for a long. Both of their eyes got stuck to each other and God only knows when Titli had held the hand of Krishna. She looked into his eyes for a long time. Slowly and gradually, Krishna made some gestures to take his hands back. Now suddenly Titli came back to her real life, looked extremely hesitant, and awkward, and immediately left his hand with a repeated sorry. Krishna didn't tell anything rather he was looking amused. He smiled looking at Titli and softly parted her sprained hairs from her forehead. Titli just closed his eyes with a deep breath. This was the softest indication of passion. Krishna took her in arms gently and kissed her, and tried to suck her breath. Titli released herself into Krishna's arm. Slowly and softly, Krishna put his hand down, Titli felt his fingers like the strokes of a paintbrush pouring the colors inside, sucking out the water out of an almost dried waterfall. Titli just closed her eyes and expanded her body ready to be painted. Krishna was the best to play with colors over her body, as someone was not only painting but playing music in her body and she was flowing like a river from the rock-solid mountain. Titli enjoyed all the strokes Krishna painted on her body. It was like the primitive language of the body, the melody of union she was feeling in her body. Krishna's touch on Titli's body was relaxing, and rejuvenating, it was a warm, melting soft touch of the wax around her body. Krishna and Tili enjoyed the physical pleasure to the utmost and ultimate. They both were floating in the fluffiness of full pleasure. Maybe for Krishna, it was not the first time but for Titli, the first time she discovered the body. She never knew her body had so many aspects to enjoy. Titli's body bloomed like a lotus, her heart was jumping like a fawn in the jungle. She was shivering like a fragrant wild creeper as Krishna was magneting her inside out. They made love for short prolonged hours without a single word. They had each other as the morning grass drinks the droplets of the early dew, as the honeybees suck the nectar from the flower. They both were feeling empty, fulfilled, refilled, and rejuvenated.

"Didi...! Didi! Titli regained her stream of consciousness at the call of the eleven-year-old boy of the gardener." bhaiya called you at security's number. Your phone is switched off for a long, so he called here to ask if you are here or not." Titli felt a sudden jolt of current in her body and mind. She tucked her saree and somehow managed to overlap the stairs. She just picked up the phone in a crushed and sobbing voice.' Krishna, Krishna, where are you? "Krishna's voice was quite flat and stabled' Titli! I knew that you would search for me. I called you from my exhibition'' After another few hours everyone found Titli extremely happy as she found her Krishna back. The old gardener of the plot used to visit the terrace sometimes with some saplings or fertilizer. The old gardener saw both of them talking, sitting, to having tea together on the balcony many times. He knew when the Mogra would bloom. So, he kept on moving towards the terrace with his pale blue, half-broken bucket. The time Titli wiped her happy tears and started to follow him as she already knew, she had to wait for her artist for more than a long, so she wanted to sit on the terrace just beside the Mogra plants.

THE END

A SEARCH OF HER OWN: FINDING RITABHARI

Ritu was feeling cold, extremely cold. Her eyes were full of tears, her vision was blurry. Though she wanted to hold a branch cozy, and tight she couldn't. Her hand didn't reach higher. The hullabaloo of the fresh young butterflies pushed her away from a very near distance. She was feeling a trance. She was feeling the tight flow of her heartbeat. She wanted to talk to someone but couldn't find anyone. Ritu started to walk slowly. She badly needed a glass of water and a companion. Nearly she found the canteen. By the gesture, she asked for a glass of water. A young boy gave it to her. Ritu was looking at the tree. It was a jamun tree. When she came to the college it was short neither too leafy nor shady. But today it is. It was giving shade to all the young butterflies who had stepped into the college. Ritu hasn't visited anything for the last twenty years. She plunged herself into family life. A few battles she won, a few battles she lost. One sunny morning in front of her mirror she discovered her gray hair lines. Ritu didn't have any friends then. For the last few years, she has been managing a few. Ritu didn't waste a single moment to ping them. Sometimes they respond, sometimes they don't but Ritu tries to make some bridges. Arpit and Mrinalini responded. Initially, she used to chat with them but they all were busy. Ritu also was in an IT company and the mother of a girl. She could not even count the days she had crossed between the two stages of her life. Now when she stands in front of the mirror the silver hairlines she touches, she cares with all of her affection. She raged the battles of her life sometimes knowingly, sometimes unknowingly. The war always left a beautiful silver line in her favorite black curl of hair. Nowadays Ritu doesn't get the fresh fragrance of Mogra. She doesn't get the time to make a bun. She is not that Ritabhari anymore. The imprisonment of heavy family life had taken her far away. The trial-and-error process of do and don't change her from the core of heart. Now she is Ritu Tagalpalewar thirty-eight. The front office executive of a reputed IT company. Ritu's husband Anay Tagalpalewar is the sales manager of one of the top car companies. Iyana is their only daughter. Iyana is in grade eight now. Last week at midnight Ritu got a panic attack in her dream. It was almost 2.30 pm. In her dream, the time machine took her away from her college days. She was running around the big field of her college and shouting and calling her friend's name but suddenly she landed in a dark desert and started to sink. She was suffering from a short breath. No one was responding to her. She was all alone. At the moment she just woke up with a parched throat. She tried to call Riyana but couldn't. She sat on the bed full of sweat. She wanted to take the water bottle from the bedside table but couldn't. As usual, Anay was not there.

Whether he was there or not never mattered. Anay was a person of sound sleep. He was indifferent about all the intricate natures of Ritu. Ritu somehow managed to step out of her bed. Took the bottle and drank water up to the bottom. Then she switched on the lights and tried to relax herself. Riyana woke up at that time. "Ma! Ma! What happened? Are you fine? Iyana knocked on the door again and again. Ritu opened the door. Riyana was scared to see her mother's pale face. She took her to the wash basin and put some water on her neck and face. The rest of the nights they both spent together. When it was approaching dawn Ritu fell asleep again. The next morning as usual Riyana went to school and Ritu went to the office. Anay hardly calls in the daytime. A few, here and there meaningless talking!! Sometimes Anay is not in a position to hear anything. Sometimes Ritu is not in a position to tell anything. Ritu was suffering out of loneliness but she never expressed it. She kept herself busy throughout the lots of work but it was not working for her. For the last two years, Ritu has been trying continuously to make some friends. Whenever she used to visit shops at the nearby cafe tables or fast-food vendors' corners, she saw groups of friends sitting, chatting not that much younger than her but she used to plunge herself into the grocery checklist meet-up. She got married at the age of nineteen. Initially, Anay and she were busy as the new journey began. But slowly Ritu found they are meant to be different, which is most common and normal. Till then Riyana had seen the lights of the world. Ritu was mature enough to handle her loneliness. She indulged in her routine work. But most of the time she used to get haunted by the same dreams. Suddenly one morning she had received a ping from Shaurya. He was a professor at Business Management College. From him, Ritu came to know they were going to have a reunion at their college. Ritu couldn't even think about it. Her collage! It was ancient history to her. A history that was not only dead but a lost world also. For the last eighteen years, she has not connected to any person from our world. Anay was a good person but Ritu knew it by the course of time that Anay controlled her to be limited in family life. Ritu was treated as a donkey though she deserved to be treated like a horse. Once Riyana grew ten years old somehow Ritu managed to get a front office job in an IT-based company. Anay was careful about her limitations. So, he handled Ritu very tactfully. Slowly and gradually, he was pulling out Ritu's confidence. But Ritu raged a war everywhere. She never let her dreams die. She wanted to be emancipated. She always wanted wings but she knew very well her wings would be well trimmed by Anay. So, in a nutshell After a few years of their marriage, Ritu realized that without raging war again and again Ritu couldn't survive in Anay's family. She welcomed her high blood pressure; she welcomed her fine line wrinkles and grey hairs. With a deep breath, she continued with everything. The unpleasant situations of her family life. The unpleasant situations of her bedtime. The unpleasant trauma of her loneliness.

Sometimes when at ease breathing out position, she used to remember her School days, College days, and old free days of her life. At that time, she used to be impulsive, she used to get mad inside. After performing all the busy schedules, and some tiring and hectic moments with Riyana when she felt like dumping her body in the bed, it was time for Anay to explore her body for a lengthy time. On the first night, Ritu didn't feel the same as the last few years. To her, it was nothing but a mere process. But with the tide of time, she couldn't realize when she had started to deposit loneliness. She used to get night trauma and disturbed sleep. Anay was touring when she declared that she wanted to visit her college reunion. As usual, Anay's first reaction was the same as he was worried about Ritu. Ritu is now very much well aware of these behaviors. She cooled herself and said "My ticket is booked now. I have to go. "When Riyana was a child Ritu was bothered about every reaction of Anay. But now she is least bothered by it. Ritu packed her suitcase. Her cook was present then. She gave her all the instructions of the household. She knew Riyana could have managed a week without her. She knew Anay would behave mentally. But to Ritu, it was the most important to go. Ritu traveled to another state. When she reached her hometown, it was midday. Her mother passed away two years ago. Her father is in a wheelchair now. A caregiver girl takes care of the whole day and night. She welcomed Ritu with a smile 'Come, Didi! You came after such a long year. Dadu was missing you! 'Ritu entered. Put the suitcase silently on the floor and hugged her father. Her father was happy to see her. First time after her marriage Ritu came home alone. After a few hours, they sat and talked. Sohini was a good girl. She brought tea with Ritu's favorite biscuits. Ritu was enjoying all these. She was feeling less burdened actually. Sohini had cleaned the washroom so nicely. After a long time, she took a bath for a long time as she used to do in her college days. While bathing she put a message in her college WhatsApp group "Reached safely. Eager to meet you all. To be very honest she was not eager to meet all. She was just eager to meet the place. The places she had left almost seventeen years back. After lunch, she took a short nap. Iyana called twice. Early evening Ritu was feeling fresh. She wore a simple cotton saree.put kajal in her eyes, light lipstick. She told Sohini over the phone to bring a jasmine garland which she wrapped over her loose bun."Ah!!! It used to be my favorite!!! Ritu smelled it deeply before putting it over her bun. She looked at the mirror and smiled. She just smiled like a sweet teenage girl. Ritu was looking pretty. When she reached her college campus it was almost 5 pm but very bright. All the young crowds were roaming here and there like fluttering butterflies. She couldn't find any known face. "Strange!!!They told me they'd come here only. "Ritu reached the Canteen, took his glass of water and suddenly came out of the trance by Mrinalini 's voice" Ritu! What are you doing here!! Are you feeling good? Ritu nodded and tried to be stable. It was very dry outside and she felt more and more thirsty inside. She felt like she had glasses of water but controlled herself and reverted to a question "What about others? Has everyone reached? 'Mrinalini did not reply. She just smiled and held the hand of Ritu. Mrinalini tried to pull Ritu a little and started to walk. At the bank of the river where they all used to gather before, they reached over there. Shaurya, Souvik, Peter, Ruchika, Devjani, and Arpit were waiting there. All responded to each other in a very formal way as happens after a long time. Ritu was searching for the same coziness she used to get years back but she couldn't find it. Rather she found the pillars of grand success stories, the well-secured amount of bank balance. Men talk about their father-in-law's financial support systems and women talk about their fluffy kitty parties and children as well. Afterward, Ritu started to feel bored. She didn't want to discuss her marital life or any nook and corner of her personal life. She was finding the bird's house where she used to receive letters every day. The bird's house she found. It was broken. It had lost its polished condition. Ritu remembered her days. She did not know who was sending her the letters but the soft white surprise used to keep her body and mind thrilled. Sometimes in the first approach of monsoon, in the foggy sleepless nights, she used to cling to those letters. She used to smell those. Life was blooming then. It was holding the corners of the colors. It was stretched towards the unknown and unseen world. It used to smell unbloomed. Nowadays Ritu never feels these all.

Who will remind her? Of course, Riyana 's few frivolous measures still show her life from a different perspective but it doesn't take her to her days. Rather it reminds her very much of her leftover days. A sudden ringing over her phone split the knot of her back-and-forth thoughts..."Hello.Sohini? Yet. Yes...I will have dinner at home. No...dear it won't take that long, I will be back before 9 pm."After disconnecting her phone Ritu felt a void again inside. Her mother was very strict about her returning home, especially at night. To avoid all hazards Ritu took a quick decision of marriage with a three-month relationship with Anay. And what happened next? Did she enjoy her freedom out of the marital knot or never did she have any freedom? Not a freedom of body, soul, and mind. Ritu never dared to stand in front of the mirror to confront all the questions. Her mother wanted her to be more careful but whatever had to happen had already happened till then. Ritu got departed from her dance. Anay was indifferent but Anay's mother's sarcastic comments drained Ritu's motivation. They opened the big kitchen door in front of her. Though the chain was too soft an intelligent girl like Ritu realized the cause and effects of ruling every step. When Ritu was pregnant, she wanted to spend a few days in her hometown but they stopped her somehow. Ritu got all the comforts but lost the flow of her river. Anay's indifference repeatedly scratched her but bleeding was not allowed. When Ritu was a teenager, her father was always worried about her dates with boys and he always used to say 'I am scared what if you become trapped by those boys!!'. Ritu didn't understand then but at the complicated times of her life, she always wished to shout and say'...Ya...It is not, I am feeling trapped!!!but her voice howled amidst the dark void. She knew no one would come to rescue her. She slowly developed to forget the things she used to love. The little zones of life started to grow grey at her end. It was evening. Shiksha Vrata Mahavidyalaya's reunion meeting was about to end. Though Ritu was not feeling comfortable she finished the chitchat light-heartedly. Sohini called one more time to ask what she would like to have for dinner. Anay also made a quick and crisp call to inquire about Ritu's current status. Ritu knew Anay was like that only. If Ritu feels helpless in any situation, Anay never turns up with the excuse of his tours and travel but today when Ritu can handle her situations, he will not leave the encryption of his husband's version rather will inquire a few more. Mrinalini and the team wanted to go for dinner outside but Ritu did not like the artificial hullabaloo. Rather she liked the personal touch of Sohini. She liked that Sohini was asking for her choice. Without a disturbance, without the noise of increasing prices of vegetables, without Riyana 's endless green stories at the dinner table and Anay's undivided attention to his laptop, at least for a few days Ritu will enjoy the silence of her dinner. Till she reached home her father slept. Baba had dinner rights. She asked Sohini. 'Yes. He takes it early nowadays '. Sohini smiled with both busy hands. That was the first time Ritu had felt at home in her hometown. No one was there to ask her what, how, and when. No one was bothered by her phone calls, no one kept on observing her. She was enjoying the silence and the whistling of outdoor trees. From the creeper jasmine soft fragrance was embracing the whole balcony. Ritu loved that smell since her childhood. Ritu changed her saree and wore her nightdress. She went to visit her father's room once. He was in a deep sleep. The door was open. Sohini touched her shoulder tenderly 'Come, Didi, I have served your dinner '..'Sohini...father sleeps so early now!!' 'Yes Didi, he can't remember things nicely and doesn't even have a good vision ...all interests are in food, Hà!!'..' let's go, Didi! Your rotis are getting cold. At the dinner table, 'Ritu enjoyed roti, potato curry, and chicken, her favorite. She was licking her finger like a child, 'Sohini, when will you eat? You could have sat with me !!'. 'No Didi, I just packed my dinner. My brother is coming to pick me up.'Sohini replied with a little hesitation. 'But you told me to stay here at night too!' 'Now you came Didi. How long you will stay, I will go back homeshoring tuck her dupatta and comb her hair once. 'Good night! Take care '. Once Sohini left Ritu locked the main gate carefully. Street lights are on. Street dogs have started to bark. When Ritu was a child, she was scared of the nighttime. She couldn't share it with anyone because being a weak-hearted girl was not allowed. Both of her parents used to be very busy all the time. When she was a small girl, she wanted to sit with her mother but her mother was busy. Sitting was not allowed. When Ritu was a teenager, she used to bring decor for her home, used to shift things here and there but her father did not accept all these. To her father, Ritu's choice was not allowed. Whenever they were in front of all the relatives there were always comparisons and Ritu always used to feel alienated and eliminated. Sometimes she used to feel suffocating but opening up was not allowed. Ritu had started to hide herself in a shell but she never wanted to. She didn't even want to be anyone's mouthpiece. She had her views and voice both but raising it was not allowed. That father who had stopped the oxygen from each inch of her life is now sleeping in another room. He sits in a wheelchair No one could make out Ritu was detaching herself from them a long far away. College days opened her door temporarily. takes and mistakes both entered spontaneously. It's not like that Ritu wished for a cozy comfortable home but the daily dashing through her parents and their marital issues was taking her to the world of temporary sexual pleasures as powerful as a drug but the consequence was leading everything towards a void. She used to receive a few letters whose writer was unknown to her. She tried to enquire about it but failed to follow any source. At a state-level essay competition, she met Anay Tagalpalewar, a twenty-five-year-old boy from Nasik. It was Anay's first visit to Bengal. A few hours together and one and a half month-long distance telephonic relationship destined both of them to marriage. When a teenager tastes a drug, the world appears flowery without considering the fatal consequences. To Ritu initially, it had appeared as a flag of freedom but she didn't expect her struggles could be never-ending. Both of their parents were not happy. Ritu shifted to Nasik and became a puppet in her in-law's hand. Slowly they took away her whole existence. Who says an elixir only tastes sweet? Venom at the same time appears sweet as well as colorful too..."Bip....bip...message came and Ritu came back to her present world. Mrinalini messaged ...."Ritu, today you looked disturbed. Is everything fine? The canteen boy wants to tell you something. I hardly shared your number with a stranger boy! Why don't you go and meet him once? But be very careful. ' Ritu replied in short 'I will call you tomorrow morning Mrinu'. The next morning Ritu woke up a little late. Baba woke up till then. Even Sohini had come. Ritu woke up with a relaxed body and mind. She had a good sleep. She knows here no one is judging her. Sohini offered her a cup of bed tea with a morning fresh smile. What a lovely beginning that was! Sitting in the bed and having a cup of tea from someone's hand!!Before taking the sip Ritu closed her eyes and tried to smell. Riyana called, "Ma! I miss you. When will you come back? Ritu laughed "Riya...it's just the second day dear. don't you want your Ma to enjoy it a little? After a few minutes of affectionate talks, Riyana disconnected. Ritu brushed and became fresh. Sohini prepared puri and sabji for breakfast. Baba was busy on mobile. Maybe he was watching a video. Ritu was laughing. 'What childish behavior!'...

She called Mrinalini and told them to meet her at the College gate around eleven. She did not feel like going alone. Reaching over there Ritu ordered two glasses of lassi. The young boy was not there. His father was working in the kitchen of the canteen. After half an hour the boy came. He gave a big welcome smile to Ritu. 'Didi...here is your photo". Ritu took the photo and recognized it was taken eighteen years back at the College Fest. But who took it? She did not have a copy of the same one. A little heavy photo of a pretty young girl of nineteen. A girl wearing a maroon color full sleeve salwar suit and net white dupatta. Her long curly hair tossed over her thin waist and trying to creep it. The big bold eyes brightly were looking through something up. 'Who gave you this photo? 'Ritu was feeling excited inside. The boy smiled again and told that man who used to write letters to you but never dared to come in front of you. Mrinalini thought the boy was an extreme prankster and didn't respect elders. She was about to scold him but Ritu stopped her. 'What do you know about it, boy?'. She asked calmly. Didi, my name is Jitu. The man you are seeing inside the kitchen is not my father. My father picked me up from a dustbin and took me home. He used to live there alone. When I grew up, I could make out he was a writer, a novelist. He used to write for Television. He is a very good person. He gave me everything but he didn't hide my birth history from me. When I found out, I started part-time work along with my studies. I wanted to make my own identity and he never said anything. Didi! One day he showed me your picture. He was writing something in his studies. It was past twelve. I entered his room and asked 'Kaka! When will you sleep? 'Kaka was very absent-minded that night. He just smiled and picked up your photo from the table. Then replied "This girl never allowed me to sleep peacefully. "Telling up to this the boy took a pause and looked back to the canteen. The boy is hardly seventeen. Ritu picked the photo slowly from the table and asked "What is your Kaku's name? And why did you touch his photo without his permission? The boy was looking confused. 'But it's not Kaku's but your photo. Why don't you go and meet him? I know he loves you. 'Mrinalini became very adamant this time 'Ritu you don't know this type of boy here. He is just trying to trap you!! You nonsense lad!!! Should I call your father from the kitchen?"...But Ritu again stopped her. God only knows why she felt to trust the boy. Maybe she will get some sources of the mystery letter writer man. She returned the photo to the boy and noted down the address. Mr. Pritish Roy Chaudhury. 3/2

Chaudhury Lane XYZ. Before leaving the canteen, she didn't tell anything to the boy. Mrinalini was not happy with all these things. She again and again cautioned Ritu' Listen dear! Nowadays situations are not as good as before. People are not trustworthy. You might be in trouble. Please Don't visit any unknown place. 'That night a rush of thoughts and excitement flushed away her sleep. 'Who the man can be? What if the boy was lying about everything? Ritu didn't know when she slept.

A heavy scenario was curtained over her brain.... Ritu was lying down on his couch in her chiffon Lemmon yellow salwar suit, From the southern balcony the soft sweet breeze was opening the letter straight again and again 'When you stand in front of your mirror at night and brush your braided long hair, can you imagine my cares over your neck? The pressing of my lips at the tip of your ear? How if I change your name from Ritu to Hri...my heart?"....' Didi, get up...your phone has been ringing for a long time. Ritu woke up with a sweating dream. Riyana called. 'Poor Riyana! She missed her school bus today. As usual, Anay said he couldn't come back as he left a long distance. Riyana is in a bad mood now. She missed her school. Ritu pacified her with all possible solutions but nothing worked. Even Ritu started the day in a bad mood. Sohini came again with a sweet suggestion 'Didi...go, take a bath you will feel fresh. I will tell my brother to bring some fresh Champa flowers for you.'Sohini laughed with a sound. Even in such a few days, Sohini came to know about her choice. While taking a bath she was humming a tune of a song which she used to sing before. After a fresh bath Ritu wore a bright yellow cotton saree with a wide blue border. It's excessively hot in the daytime, best to make a ponytail. While putting on some soft touch of makeup, she didn't forget to look around her silver-grey lines of hair.'Sohini, I will be a little late today. Don't keep lunch for me.'Sohini always became a loving fellow. Just smiled and stretched her hand with a bunch of fresh pales and yellow Champa. Ritu quickly managed to push aside her tied hair. Ritu didn't take a taxi. She was enjoying herself inside the bus. The crowd, the smoke, the cracked typical voice of the vendors everything she was enjoying alone. When she found the address of Chaudhury Lane it was almost eleven thirty. A middle-aged elegant and sophisticated man opened the door. The man was wearing denim and a white handloom kurti. Cleaned shaved, bright eyes, and tall tight appearance. He was wearing a high-power frame and looked towards Ritu deeply. "Hello! I am looking for Mr. Pritish Roy Chaudhury. "The man welcomed her spontaneously and led them towards the drawing room. With a hand gesture, he requested her to sit. Ritu was feeling quite hesitant and managed herself to be seated., 'I am Ritu, Ritu Bhattacharjee '. I recently came from Behala but I have stayed in Nasik for nine thirteen years. The man sat in front of her. All with dignity in voice he replied 'Yes, right place you are in and Myself Pritish Raychaudhuri. And if I am not wrong my foster son Jitu has given you, my address. 'The man was looking confident but Ritu was feeling nervous. He was not looking for fraud or something at all but Ritu had never seen him before.' A! Ahed! Ritu tried to clear out her throat and said 'Jitu was telling you to have a picture of mine but I don't remember any. 'Pritish laughed a little louder 'I do have more than one Ritabhari but you don't remember because you don't know, I didn't want Ritabhari to know a single bit of Pritish. 'Only you wanted me to read your letters by and from unknown sources!!! Was it all? 'Why did you cut your name, and why did you cut your hair? 'Pritish asked very politely but Ritu was feeling very angry inside 'Why didn't you turn up in front of me ever?" I won't lie to you Ritabhari, I was a teenager when I used to write to you. I hardly had a purpose in my life but when I found myself eligible, I collected your address and I reached your home. Honestly, they didn't even talk to me nicely. I didn't mind. At least I came to know Ritabhari Bhattacharjee was happily married and became Mrs. Ritu Tagalpalewar. I saw you on social media but it was late. Sorry, I couldn't give you anything other than those letters. Ritu felt to shout and scratch the man 'That's how you compelled me to make love with silence, with darkness, with breezes and so many but her voice choked. Somehow, she controlled herself from a burst. Pritish was looking at her deeply and asked 'Ritabhari, will you have tea? Or coffee? Ritu came to consciousness.' hand…ohh, yet. Yes…tea fine '. The man smiled and went indoors. Ritu was looking around the room. Self-self-books everywhere. Nice indoor plants, artistic sense everywhere, Sober host! What's not? Everything! Everything that she used to dream about at a young age. Everything which she hankered after her marital life. Pritish entered after a few minutes with two cups of tea in his hand. 'Thanks! Ritu took one and sat again. Jitu was telling me you are a writer. What do you write? 'Whatever my production house expects me to do!! I have been working for ten years on tele platforms. ' Pritish shrugged a little. Ritu observed that Pritish is quite handsome, maybe a little younger than her.'So..how was your college reunion? Jitu was telling me about it. '..'Yes, all good. Met all after a long time. 'Both of them tried to be a little formal, specifically Ritu. Almost an hour they took on some common chit-chat. Weather in Nashik, Ritu's job with Riyana, Anay's busy schedules, everything. Gradually Ritu also came to know that Jitu is in grade eleven now. He just helps Naren Samanta to take care of the payment department of the canteen and manage his pocket money too. Suddenly Ritu asked 'So in this house only you two stay, right? I mean. I just...didn't you get married?" Yes, of course, I did Ritabhari. I see you have a poor observation; Pritish lowered his voice a little. 'You didn't even recognize my many beautiful wives and he looked back towards his bookshelves at a time. Ritu tried to laugh falsely. She was feeling emotionally desperate but she wanted to hide it from the British. Women feel cowardly to show how destitute they become from the inside. Society loves enriched women, not a lonely one. Any way Ritu had obtained expertise to hide her feelings. In between Anay called, Riyana

Mrinalini called, and Sohini called. Ritu talked to all of them dutifully. It was almost two, Ritu wanted to come back but Pritish stopped her for lunch. By this time Jitu also came back. The three of them had lunch together. Ritu liked the bondage between Jitu and Pritish. Jitu told Pritish' Kaku! Why didn't you show her our roof balcony?' 'A nice idea indeed! 'Pritish took Ritu to the roof garden where in the bright daylight mogra, jasmine, sunflower and a few fragrant unknown creepers were blooming smiling. 'Nice garden….' Ritu commented a little jovial. 'I love flowers!!!' ' And I know it very well '. Pritish replied. Ritu sat over there quietly for a long time. Pritish didn't disturb her. He left towards his terrace room. Ritu was thinking of all the letters from Pritish. The words engraved over there were able to bloom her as he bloomed all the flowers in his garden. Even Pritish never knew his words filled so many silent moments of her life. They used to wrap her in a cozy blanket on her sleepless nights. Sohini 's phone call again took her back from a long-cherished graveyard. 'Yes…Sohini, I will come back before tea time.

.'..Pritish wanted to drop her but Ritu refused. She took a taxi and loosened her body inside. She was feeling tired. The sun was about to set with an all-along rush of unseen and unknown. Who knows the next morning? Who has seen tomorrow? Time takes time from time to time. What does it leave behind? Elixir or poison? Ritu just texted a message to Pritish '...Do you remember, long back in one of your letters you wrote….You used to be missing out of the crowd of twenty for one me…So it was. Now I feel not even a single one still when I am twenty. And…more and more…What do you think? Am I setting?

While having the tea, Ritu booked her ticket. Poor Riyana was suffering to manage. She had to return soon. Before leaving all my old friends went on a day trip. That day Ritu didn't feel alienated, rather she was looking happy. Of course, she had spent a few days with herself, with Ritabhari. Sohini made her happy. She cried when Ritu was leaving. Ritu shopped for her. Sohini loved those items. After collecting the boarding pass Ritu called Anay. Though he was busy in important meetings, he at least remembered Ritu was returning. On the flight, Ritu didn't forget to message her old friends formally, typically. She fastened her belt tight. She was feeling cold. Ritabhari was going far away from her. The air hostess announced in a sweet voice to switch off the passenger's phone. Before switching it off Ritu sends the last message to Pritish 'Ritabhari is leaving your city today, love for Jitu. Bye'...The flight departed on time and Ritu saw down the window, the glowing diamond necklace light hanging around her old city was getting faded timid and dimmed. It faded, faded, and faded until it turned into a void.

THE END